D0545838

FOR PETER AND MATHEW

This edition published by Parragon Books Ltd in 2014
Parragon
Chartist House
15-17 Trim Street
Bath BA1 1HA, UK
www.parragon.com

Published by arrangement with Gullane Children's Books

Text and illustrations © Sarah Massini 2012

All rights reserved. No part of this publication may be reproduced, stored in a retrieval system, or transmitted in any form or by any means, electronic, mechanical, photocopying, recording or otherwise, without the prior permission of the copyright holder.

ISBN: 978-1-4723-3203-5

Printed in China.

TRIXIE TEN

SARAH MASSINI

PaRRagon

Bath • New York • Singapore • Hong Kong • Cologne • Delhi
Melbourne • Amsterdam • Johannesburg • Shenzhen

This is
Trixie TEN.
She has nine brothers and sisters.
She thinks they are very annoying and this is why.

Wanda ONE
is always sneezing.

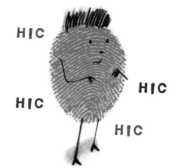

Thomas TWO
has hiccups.

Theo THREE
burps and parps.

Florence FOUR
is always a-giggle.

Felix FIVE
laughs very loudly.

Scarlett SIX
bumps into things.

Sam SEVEN
is always surprised.

Emily EIGHT
always has a runny
nose and never ever
a handkerchief.

Nathaniel NINE
is the most annoying of all.
He is always pretending
to be a lion.

At night-time, to make sure they are all safe and sound and tucked up in their ten little beds, Trixie and her brothers and sisters count themselves in:

Wanda
ONE

Thomas
TWO

Theo
THREE

Florence
FOUR

Felix
FIVE

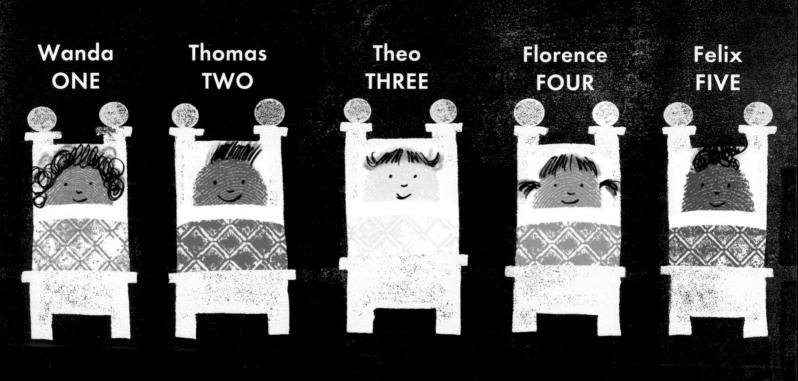

Scarlett
SIX

Sam
SEVEN

Emily
EIGHT

Nathaniel
NINE

Trixie
TEN

"**Nine** brothers and sisters are **so noisy!**" sighs Trixie.

It isn't any quieter during the day.
"**Nine** brothers and sisters are **too noisy!**" sighs Trixie.
"And they take up **too much room!**"

But one day, Trixie had an idea.
She packed some things into
a useful bag. She packed:

ONE useful torch,

ONE useful teddy,

ONE useful blanket.

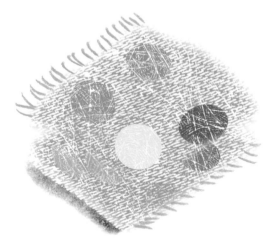

HIC
HIC
HIC
HAHA
TCHOOOOOoo
ROAR
OW

And when no one was looking,
she crept away in search of
somewhere quiet.

She walked and walked until. . .

BUBBLE

BUBBLE

BUBBLE

BUBBLE

. . . she came to a stream.

But it certainly wasn't quiet - it was full of bubbling fish!
'These are my **nine** brothers and sisters,' explained a fish.
Trixie counted them.
'You're **very noisy** . . . for fish!'
'That's just the way we are!' the fish laughed proudly.

Trixie said goodbye to the fish.
She walked and walked until. . .

BUBBLE

BUBBLE

BUBBLE

BUBBLE

. . . she came to a meadow.

'What a lot of rabbits!' said Trixie.
They took up **so much room!**
"These are my **ninety-nine** brothers and sisters,"
said the rabbit happily.

Trixie counted them.
"Maybe **nine** brothers and sisters isn't so
many after all!" she thought.

Trixie said goodbye to the rabbits.
She walked and walked until. . .

. . . she found a
big, empty, quiet place.

Night time came.
Silent and still.
Trixie got out her useful torch. She hugged her useful teddy
and she counted the spots on her useful blanket.

And she began to think about
Wanda and Thomas and Theo and Florence and Felix,
Scarlett, Sam, Emily and Nathaniel.
She wished she had someone to talk to.
She wished she wasn't **so alone**. . .

Meanwhile Trixie's brothers and sisters
were counting themselves into bed.
Was everyone all tucked up?
Was everyone safe and sound?

Wanda
ONE

Thomas
TWO

Theo
THREE

Florence
FOUR

Felix
FIVE

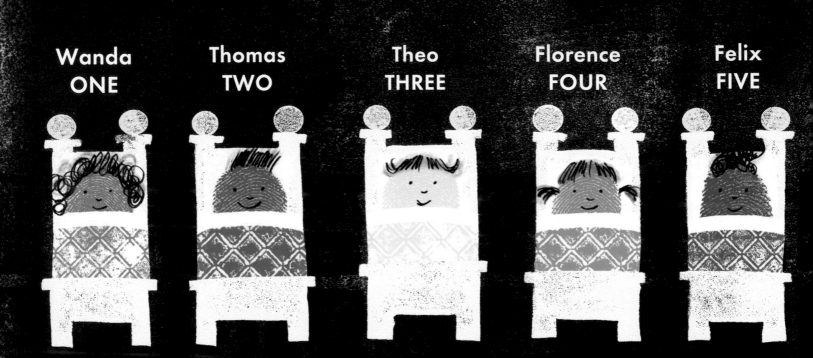

Scarlett
SIX

Sam
SEVEN

Emily
EIGHT

Nathaniel
NINE

...?

"Where is Trixie TEN?"

ROARAH HA HA HA HA BURP WOW WOW

RP WOW BURP WOW HIC

TEE HEE HEE

SNIFF

OW SNIFF WOW PARP

HIC

ATCHOOOO HIC

It was very dark outside.
It was silent and still and
very, very scary.
But they bravely went in search of Trixie Ten.
They walked and walked until . . .

"**It's me!**" cried Trixie,
switching on her useful torch.
"**I heard you coming!**"
she laughed.

"Please come back home!" said her
nine brothers and sisters.
"We missed you!"
"I missed you too,"
said Trixie. "**A lot!**"
And they made their
noisy way back
home . . .

... and counted themselves into bed:

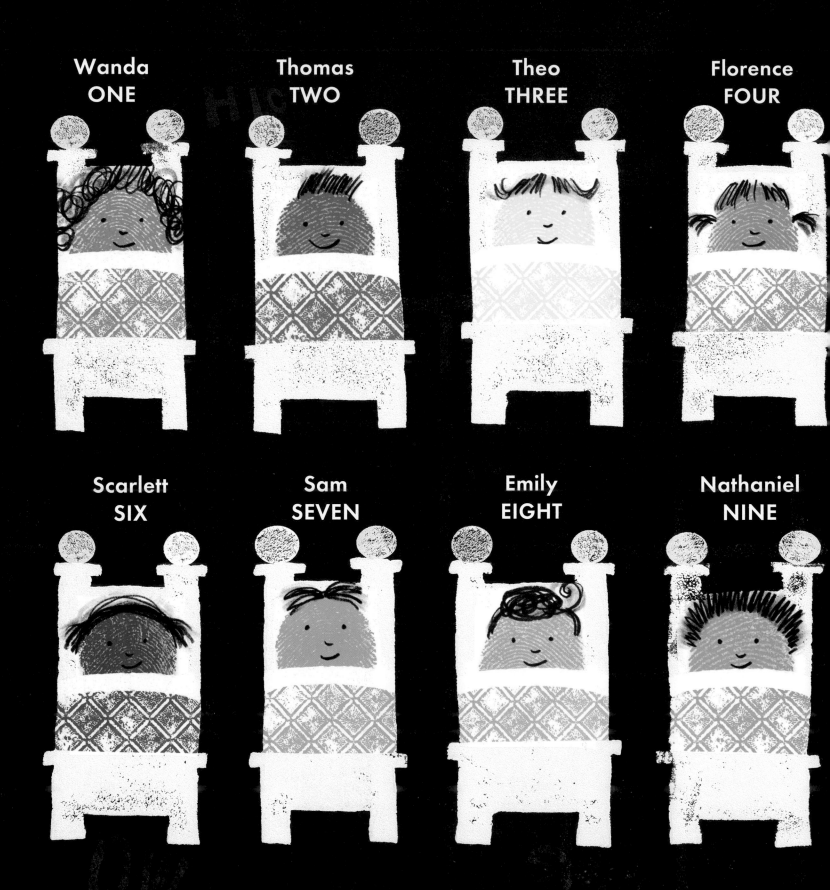

Wanda
ONE

Thomas
TWO

Theo
THREE

Florence
FOUR

Scarlett
SIX

Sam
SEVEN

Emily
EIGHT

Nathaniel
NINE

Felix
FIVE

HIC
HIC
HA HA HA
BANG
ROAR
TEE HEE HEE

Trixie
TEN

It was just as **noisy** as usual.
"But that's the way we are,"
thought Trixie.

And she put on some useful,
noise-proof head-phones,
and drifted happily off to sleep . . .